THE GREAT HAIR ROBBERY

ALAN HORSFIELD
AND CONNAH BRECON

Lothian
BOOKS

Thomas C. Lothian Pty Ltd
132 Albert Road, South Melbourne, Victoria 3205
www.lothian.com.au

National Library of Australia
Cataloguing-in-Publication data:

Horsfield, Alan.
The great hair robbery.
For primary school children.

ISBN 0 7344 0517 0

1. Brecon, Connah.
II. Title. (Series: Start-ups).

A823.3

Cover design by Michelle Mackintosh
Text design by Paulene Meyer
Printed in Australia by Hyde Park Press

CHAPTER ONE

Nellie woke up early. Soon it would
be Christmas and
she was getting
excited. Today
Santa Claus would
be in the Big Store.

She hopped out of bed and grabbed her hairbrush that lay on the dressing table nearby.

She looked at herself in the mirror, as she did every morning. Nellie had silky, long, silver-blond hair, which she wore in a ponytail. She was very fond of her hair.

She was just about to start brushing when, to her horror, she saw she had no hair. No hair at all! She couldn't believe it.

Nellie ran her fingers over her bald scalp several times, not believing

what her eyes were telling her and not believing what her fingers could feel. Her scalp was as bare as her father's bald patch!

She grabbed a pink tissue from her lace-covered tissue box and wiped the mirror very hard — just in case it wasn't working properly.

Still she had no hair. She also had no eyebrows.

Maybe they fell off in bed. She quickly looked under the sheets, under the pillow and even under the bed.

No hair and no eyebrows were to be seen anywhere. She was getting ready to panic.

Nellie rushed out of her bedroom and into the kitchen. Her mother and father were sitting at the breakfast bar looking very sad.

'We know, dear. We know,' said her mother glumly.

Both her mother and father were completely bald. Her mother was close to crying. Just the day before she had been to the hairdresser to have a perm and a black rinse put in her hair.

Her eyebrows had been fine black lines over her eyes.

Her father didn't look quite so worried. He didn't have much hair anyway. Just a little band of thinning hair around the sides and back of his head. Nothing on top.

What gave Nellie a surprise was that her father's beard had gone.

She had never, in her whole life, seen him without his grey beard. She would not have recognised him if she had passed him in the street.

Now he was rubbing his bare chin and shaking his pink, bald head.

Nellie sat down with her parents, but no-one had anything to say. They were all in a state of shock.

They were not game enough to go out into the street.

Finally, Nellie had an idea. She put on her parka with a big hood, which almost covered her face.

It was quite cool after all! No-one would know she didn't have any hair. She did so want to see Santa Claus!

Her dad nodded sadly. It was a good idea for Nellie, but he couldn't wear a parka to work. He was a bank manager!

What a surprise Nellie got when she walked down the main street. It looked like everyone had lost their hair.

Many people had big hats on or scarves over their heads, but

everyone else knew they didn't have any hair!

People were standing on street corners and in front of shops talking softly about the terrible thing that had occurred.

No-one could say how it had happened.

CHAPTER TWO

Nellie saw Mr Short, the barber, standing outside his shop. He was looking very sad indeed. He was bald anyway, but now he had no customers.

He had a sign in his window.

Sale

Hair remover –
five bottles for the price
of one!
Hair restorer –
$150 a bottle!
Brushes, combs, clips
and ribbons at
give-away prices!

Now everyone was too upset to
even think about buying hair restorer.
She walked past the electrical
shop. It had a sign in the window too.

Going cheap!

Hair dryers, half price.

Save – save – save.

Hair clippers –
make us an offer!

No-one was buying.

What had happened to every-one's hair?

She met Sergeant Smithers just as she was passing a new shop.

25

A big sign on the window read:

Opening soon
Kay Calvin's Wig Shop

Come to Kay Calvin for wigs

for all occasions. All sizes.

Wigs for young and old.

Wigs for men and women.

Wigs for judges, butchers

and candlestick makers.

Sergeant Smithers didn't see the sign. He had his police cap pulled down tight on his head. He was looking very confused.

'You know what Nellie, I think someone has stolen everyone's hair.'

Policemen always suspect something.

'I don't know how, and I don't care how. Everyone wants their hair back. We should do something about locating it!' said the sergeant.

Nellie just shook her head. What could she say?

Sergeant Smithers started wandering off, muttering, 'And the Police Chief won't even come out of his office!'

Nellie continued towards the Big Shop. It was covered in decorations and lights, and big Santa Claus faces with long, white hair and bushy, white whiskers. She was

getting so excited, she almost forgot
that she had no hair!

Just as she was about to enter
the big revolving door she saw a
strange sight.

Down the street rode a man on a penny-farthing. He was wearing black clothes. A long, black cloak flowed in the wind behind him. He had long, black trousers on his skinny legs, a big, black top hat and shiny, black boots with high heels.

And he had long, black hair down to his shoulders, black whiskers and a thin, black moustache that turned up at the ends. He looked like a wizard.

That's odd, thought Nellie, I haven't seen a wizard for ages.

Then the doors turned and she went into the shop.

The shop was in turmoil. Bald parents were in a big crush all over the toy department. Bald babies were crying everywhere. Little bald children were clinging to parents' legs. No-one was happy.

Nellie was too small to see what had caused the confusion. A bald-headed mother, pushing a pram, escaped from the crowd and was rushing for the doors. She looked very displeased.

'Excuse me,' said Nellie in a very respectful voice. 'What has happened?'

'What has happened! I'll tell you what has happened. Santa Claus won't come out to greet the children — or get his picture taken. He won't come out because he hasn't got any hair, just like everyone else! He has lost his hair!'

A Santa Claus without his long, white hair and white beard! It was terrible!

The lady had hardly slowed down to speak to Nellie. Before Nellie

could thank her, she had disappeared

into the street, her face held high.

This could be a sad Christmas.

CHAPTER THREE

It was then that Nellie remembered
the man in black. He had hair and
Santa Claus had none. There was
something very strange going on,
but what could a little girl do? Nellie
walked out into the street trying hard
to think of something.

Then she saw *it*.

Morcomb & B. Rush

Private Detectives

We catch stealers of

dreams, great train

robbers, cattle rustlers,

and accept rewards.

No job is too big or too small!

Our motto:

Give the rest the brush,

come to Morcomb and Rush.

She didn't have to do anything — she could get the detectives to find the lost hair!

In their office, which had a big city map on the wall, she told the detectives what she thought they should do. The detectives sat behind their desk and rubbed their chins. Then they both had a sip of coffee out of rather grubby mugs.

Nellie told them about the man on the penny-farthing. 'He was tall and thin and wearing black clothes. He had a long, black cloak; long, black trousers; and skinny legs. He was wearing a big, black top hat and shiny, black boots with high heels!'

This made Mr Rush look up.

'And he had long, black hair down to his shoulders, black whiskers, and a thin, black moustache that turned up at the ends.' Nellie said triumphantly.

'We need a clue!' declared Mr Morcomb. 'Er, did this gentleman have any special features? You know, scars or tattoos, so we could recognise him. Did you happen to get the number of his, er … bike? Not much use if we can't put out a description of his, er, getaway vehicle.'

43

'It's not much use to us if we can't identify him,' said Mr Rush rubbing his chin. He looked as if he was exploring for whiskers.

'Well,' said Nellie, 'he does have hair.'

The detectives looked at her as if waiting for her to explain what she meant.

'He had hair! Black hair!' said Nellie, somewhat exasperated.

The detectives looked at each other and grinned, and together they both said, 'Brilliant!'

'We can put out a description over the radio,' said Mr Morcomb.

'And on TV too!' said Mr Rush.

'If anyone sees him they can ring us at our office,' they both said.

'And we can rush to the spot — and nab him!' added Mr Rush.

By lunchtime all the radio and TV stations were asking people to help.

Almost as soon as they started, the telephone rang.

Mr Rush grabbed it. Someone had seen the man with hair, black hair. They gave his position.

Mr Rush put a big, blue pin in the city map. 'We have our man! Let's go out and pick him up. To the van!' He looked pleased with himself.

They were just heading for the door when the phone rang again. Mr Morcomb grabbed it. Someone else had seen the man. They gave his position.

Mr Morcomb put another blue pin in the city map, just above the first pin. 'Now we've got our man! Let's go!' He looked pleased with himself.

49

They were just heading for the door when the phone rang again. Mr Rush grabbed it. Someone else had seen the man. They gave his position.

Mr Rush put another blue pin in the city map, just above the second pin. 'Now we've got our man! Now we can go!' He looked pleased with himself.

Then the phone rang again. Another pin went in the city map.

'Oh dear,' said Mr Morcomb, 'we will never get him. He keeps moving all over the place!'

The phone rang again and again and again.

Blue pins went in the map again and again and again.

The detectives looked sad and defeated.

'So much for that good idea,' muttered Mr Rush.

Nellie looked at the city map. 'Look at the map,' she said. 'All the blue pins are going in a line along the road to the old sports ground. I bet that's where the man with hair is going.'

The detectives' eyes lit up. 'That's right! Let's go. Nellie you can, er, mind the phone.'

There was no way Nellie was going to mind the phone. She was going in the van with the detectives.

When the phone rang again the office was empty.

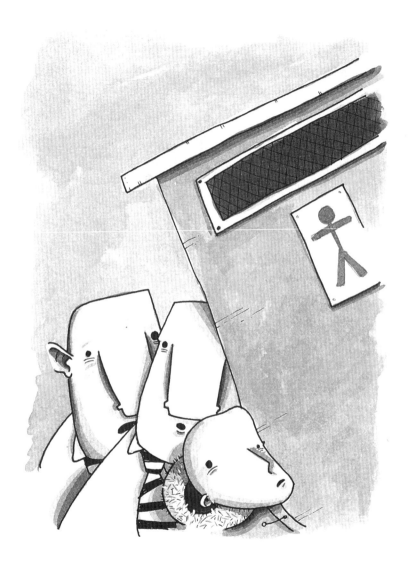

CHAPTER FOUR

It took just a few minutes to get to the old sports ground. Mr Rush had called the police on his mobile phone as they raced down the wide streets. It really was a police matter.

At the old sports ground they hid behind the dressing rooms just as the man in black sailed in on his penny-farthing. Sirens wailed in the distance.

'Why it's the master criminal, Calvin Kay!' whispered Mr Morcomb.

Mr Rush whispered to Nellie: 'Calvin Kay is the Great Train Robber. He had half a dozen trains hidden in the old stadium before they put him away.'

'You said his name was Calvin Kay. Do you know there is a new wig shop opening soon called Kay Calvin?'

'Sounds suspicious,' murmured Mr Morcomb slowly.

'And do you know what Calvin means?' whispered Nellie as Calvin Kay got closer.

'This is not the time for a quiz,' said Mr Rush sternly but quietly.

'Listen! It means "bald"!' hissed Nellie. She had seen it in a book of names. 'It all fits together!'

They both looked at her in amazement.

'You know, you could be right,' Mr Rush said thoughtfully.

'Here he comes!' called Mr Morcomb.

As Calvin Kay drifted by on the penny-farthing, they all jumped out. Calvin Kay got such a shock he swerved widely and headed straight for the dressing-room door.

He smashed right through it and ended up in a heap on the floor.

Then the Police Chief and Sergeant Smithers arrived, sirens wailing.

They all rushed to the dressing room together.

There was Calvin Kay lying in a tangle of hair and whiskers. He couldn't get up.

Sergeant Smithers arrested him on the spot! 'Now we know all about the great hair robbery,' he said.

And they did!

Calvin Kay had used a spell to steal everyone's hair. He then made the stolen hair into wigs to sell in the Kay Calvin Wig Shop. He had known that everyone would want to buy a wig. He had thought he was going to be rich!

The thing about hair is, when you cut it, it grows again. Within a few weeks, most men and some women had their hair back.

Nellie's father had his little band of thin hair around the back of his head in a few days!

Santa Claus sneaked out and bought a big, white wig and a pretend white beard while he waited for his real hair to grow, so he could go back into the shop and tell boys and girls what they might get for Christmas.

Do you know, sometimes now he will wear a wig and pretend beard to remind himself of the time when he had no hair at all!